GOSCINNY AND UDERZO
PRESENT
An Asterix Adventure

ASTERIX
THE
LEGIONARY

Written by RENÉ GOSCINNY *and Illustrated by* ALBERT UDERZO

Translated by Anthea Bell *and* Derek Hockridge

Orion
Children's Books

Asterix titles available now

ORION CHILDREN'S BOOKS

This revised edition first published in 2004 by Orion Books Ltd
This edition published in 2016 by Hodder and Stoughton

1 3 5 7 9 10 8 6 4 2

ASTERIX®-OBELIX®
© 1967 GOSCINNY/UDERZO
Revised edition and English translation © 2004 Hachette Livre
Original title: *Astérix légionnaire*
Exclusive licensee: Hachette Children's Group
Translators: Anthea Bell and Derek Hockridge
Typography: Bryony Newhouse

The right of René Goscinny and Albert Uderzo to be identified as the authors of this work
has been asserted by them in accordance with the Copyright, Designs and Patents Act 1988.

A CIP record for this book is available from the British Library

ISBN 978-0-7528-6620-8 (cased)
ISBN 978-0-7528-6621-5 (paperback)
ISBN 978-1-4440-1317-7 (ebook)

Printed in China
The paper and board used in this book are from well-managed forests and other responsible sources.

Orion Children's Books
An imprint of Hachette Children's Group, part of Hodder and Stoughton
Carmelite House, 50 Victoria Embankment
London EC4Y 0DZ
An Hachette UK Company

www.hachette.co.uk
www.asterix.com
www.hachettechildrens.co.uk

GAULISH VILLAGE

COMPENDIUM

LAUDANUM

AQUARIUM

TOTORUM

ARMORICA

BELGICA

LUTETIA

SPQR

GAUL
(ROMAN CONQUEST)
50 BC

CELTICA

AQUITANIA

PROVINCIA

THE YEAR IS 50 BC. GAUL IS ENTIRELY OCCUPIED BY THE
ROMANS. WELL, NOT ENTIRELY ... ONE SMALL VILLAGE OF
INDOMITABLE GAULS STILL HOLDS OUT AGAINST THE INVADERS.
AND LIFE IS NOT EASY FOR THE ROMAN LEGIONARIES WHO
GARRISON THE FORTIFIED CAMPS OF TOTORUM, AQUARIUM,
LAUDANUM AND COMPENDIUM ...

ASTERIX, THE HERO OF THESE ADVENTURES. A SHREWD, CUNNING LITTLE WARRIOR, ALL PERILOUS MISSIONS ARE IMMEDIATELY ENTRUSTED TO HIM. ASTERIX GETS HIS SUPERHUMAN STRENGTH FROM THE MAGIC POTION BREWED BY THE DRUID GETAFIX . . .

OBELIX, ASTERIX'S INSEPARABLE FRIEND. A MENHIR DELIVERY MAN BY TRADE, ADDICTED TO WILD BOAR. OBELIX IS ALWAYS READY TO DROP EVERYTHING AND GO OFF ON A NEW ADVENTURE WITH ASTERIX – SO LONG AS THERE'S WILD BOAR TO EAT, AND PLENTY OF FIGHTING. HIS CONSTANT COMPANION IS DOGMATIX, THE ONLY KNOWN CANINE ECOLOGIST, WHO HOWLS WITH DESPAIR WHEN A TREE IS CUT DOWN.

GETAFIX, THE VENERABLE VILLAGE DRUID, GATHERS MISTLETOE AND BREWS MAGIC POTIONS. HIS SPECIALITY IS THE POTION WHICH GIVES THE DRINKER SUPERHUMAN STRENGTH. BUT GETAFIX ALSO HAS OTHER RECIPES UP HIS SLEEVE . . .

CACOFONIX, THE BARD. OPINION IS DIVIDED AS TO HIS MUSICAL GIFTS. CACOFONIX THINKS HE'S A GENIUS. EVERY-ONE ELSE THINKS HE'S UNSPEAKABLE. BUT SO LONG AS HE DOESN'T SPEAK, LET ALONE SING, EVERYBODY LIKES HIM . . .

FINALLY, VITALSTATISTIX, THE CHIEF OF THE TRIBE. MAJESTIC, BRAVE AND HOT-TEMPERED, THE OLD WARRIOR IS RESPECTED BY HIS MEN AND FEARED BY HIS ENEMIES. VITALSTATISTIX HIMSELF HAS ONLY ONE FEAR, HE IS AFRAID THE SKY MAY FALL ON HIS HEAD TOMORROW. BUT AS HE ALWAYS SAYS, TOMORROW NEVER COMES.

LATER...
GOOD HUNTING, OBELIX, EH?
HMMM?

LET'S GO AND COOK THE BOARS RIGHT AWAY. THEN WE CAN HAVE A NICE REST!

HEY, OBELIX! WHERE ARE THOSE BOARS?

MMPH... BOARS? WHAT BOARS?

OH, YOU MEAN THESE BOARS...
GRRRRRRRRR!

SOON AFTERWARDS...
AAAH! THAT WAS GOOD!

2A

NOW THEN, OBELIX, EAT UP YOUR THIRD BOAR. THEN WE'LL HAVE OUR REST.
NO, THANKS. SOMEHOW I DON'T FEEL HUNGRY ANY MORE. — DEEP SIGH —

OBELIX! ARE YOU ILL?
NO, NO... DEEPER SIGH

DEEPEST SIGH

COME QUICK, O DRUID GETAFIX! I'M WORRIED! OBELIX WON'T EAT UP HIS BOAR. HE SAYS HE DOESN'T FEEL HUNGRY!
DID HE HAVE ANYTHING ELSE FIRST?

JUST TWO BOARS.
TWO BOARS... THAT HARDLY COUNTS. BETTER HAVE A LOOK AT HIM!

2B

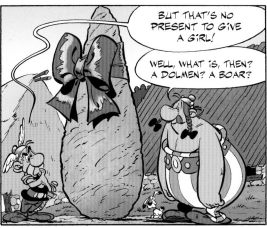

9

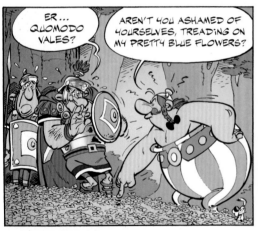

A MESSAGE FOR YOU, PANACEA!

HULLO! THAT'S POSTALDISTRIX THE POSTMAN!

YOU DON'T MIND IF I READ IT NOW?

NOT AT ALL!

OH! BY BELISAMA!

WHAT'S THE MATTER? IS IT BAD NEWS?

READ THAT!

I'VE JUST GOT TIME TO CARVE A WORD. THE ROMANS MADE ME JOIN THE LEGION. WE'RE OFF TO AFRICA. FAREWELL FOR EVER

TRAGICOMIX

WHO'S TRAGICOMIX, PANACEA?

WE GOT TO KNOW EACH OTHER AT CONDATUM. WE'RE ENGAGED...

8A

DON'T CRY, PANACEA. WE'LL GO AND FIND TRAGICOMIX FOR YOU. WON'T WE, ASTERIX?

I'LL SAY! WE'LL BRING HIM BACK EVEN IF WE HAVE TO GO ALL THE WAY TO AFRICA! LET'S GO AND SEE OUR CHIEF VITALSTATISTIX, OBELIX!

OBELIX, I'M PROUD OF YOU! YOU WERE REALLY BRAVE! WHEN YOU HEARD PANACEA WAS ENGAGED YOU DIDN'T EVEN...

BOOHOOHOOO! I'M SO UNHAPPY!

8B

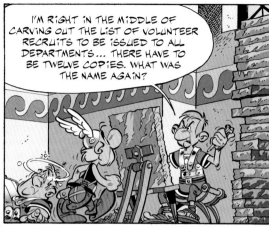
I'M RIGHT IN THE MIDDLE OF CARVING OUT THE LIST OF VOLUNTEER RECRUITS TO BE ISSUED TO ALL DEPARTMENTS... THERE HAVE TO BE TWELVE COPIES. WHAT WAS THE NAME AGAIN?

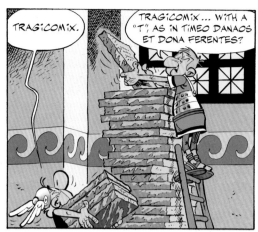
TRAGICOMIX.

TRAGICOMIX... WITH A "T", AS IN TIMEO DANAOS ET DONA FERENTES?

AH, HERE WE ARE... TRAGICOMIX HAS LEFT WITH A CONVOY. AT THIS MOMENT HE'S DUE TO TAKE SHIP AT MASSILIA WITH REINFORCEMENTS FOR CAESAR. THEY'RE OFF TO AFRICA.

AFRICA... HMMM...

OBELIX! COME HERE!

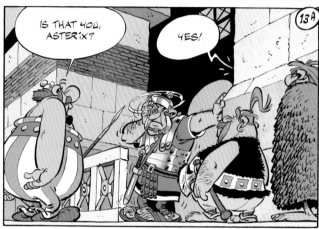
IS THAT YOU, ASTERIX?

YES!

13 A

COMING!

NOW THEN! LET'S BE POLITE!

WHAM!

?!!

TRAGICOMIX HAS LEFT FOR AFRICA. THE ONLY WAY TO GET HIM BACK NOW IS TO JOIN THE ROMAN ARMY.

WHAT, US? JOIN THE ROMAN ARMY? STILL, IF YOU THINK IT WOULD HELP PANACEA...

SOON AFTERWARDS...

OUCH... WHAT DID THOSE TWO HAVE AGAINST ME, ANYWAY...?

13 B

17

19

22

THE EGYPTIAN WANTS TO SEE THE MENU.

I SAY, DO YOU THINK THEY'LL HAVE BOAR?

DON'T GET ANY IDEAS! THE STRONGER THE ARMY, THE WORSE ITS FOOD IS. THAT'S WHAT KEEPS THE MEN IN A NASTY MOOD!

FLOTCH!

PLOTCH!

SLOP!

FLOTCH!

I DIDN'T THINK THE ROMAN ARMY WAS THAT STRONG!

20A

THE EGYPTIAN WANTS TO SEE THE MANAGER.

I'M NOT STAYING FOR LESS THAN SIX SESTERTII A DAY!

POSITIVELY GOTHIC, THIS FOOD!

At home people would be quartered for less!

BANG!

LOOK, NO JOKING... WHAT IS IT?

IT'S LEGIONARY RATIONS... YOU'LL BE GETTING IT EVERY DAY, CORN, BACON AND CHEESE, ALL COOKED TOGETHER TO SAVE TIME!

LET'S GO AND HAVE A WORD WITH THE COOK, ASTERIX!

JUST WHAT I WAS ABOUT TO SUGGEST MYSELF, OBELIX!

SLOUP!
SLOUP!

DELICIOUS! REALLY SPLENDID, DON'T YOU KNOW!

20B

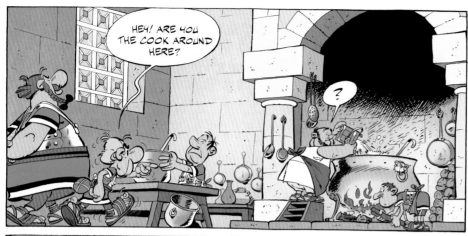

ER... NOW WE HAVE GLADIUS DRILL...

THESE ARE ONLY PRETEND SWORDS, OF COURSE, MADE OF WOOD... COME ON!

?!

WELL, COME ON! DEFEND YOURSELF!

BUT IF IT'S ONLY MADE OF WOOD...

DO AS YOU'RE TOLD, OBELIX! WE'RE ONLY WASTING TIME!!

OH, VERY WELL!

THESE ROMANS ARE CRAZY!

TCHAC!

OH NO! IF THIS GOES ON IT'LL NEVER BE READY, AND IT'LL TASTE PRETTY FUNNY TOO!

23A

THAT EVENING...

CHEER UP, DUBIUS STATUS! THE RECRUITS WILL HAVE TO BE UP AT THE CRACK OF DAWN FOR A ROUTE MARCH WITH SACKS FULL OF ROCKS. THAT'LL KEEP THEM QUIET...

JUST A SHOT OF MAGIC POTION FOR TOMORROW, AND I'M TURNING IN. WE HAVE TO BE UP EARLY!

MORE BOAR HERE!

COMING!

THAT'S A NICE THOUGHT! THEY WON'T BE QUITE SO SMART WHEN I GET THEM OUT OF BED AT DAWN TOMORROW!

BUT ONLY A FEW SHORT HOURS LATER...

WAKEY, WAAAKEY!

?

RISE AND SHINE!

COME ON EVERY-ONE!

C- C- COMING!

23B

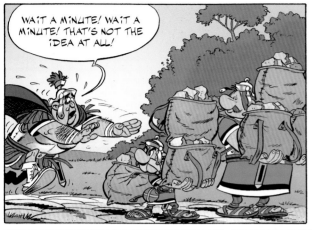

25⁹

25⁶⁰

UNDER THE COMMAND OF CENTURION NEFARIUS PURPUS, THE MEN OF THE 1ST LEGION, 3RD COHORT, 2ND MANIPLE, 1ST CENTURY, LEAVE CONDATUM...

I THINK WE'VE BEEN GOING LONG ENOUGH ... WE'LL STOP FOR A BIT...

1ST LEGION, 3RD COHORT, 2ND MANIPLE, 1ST CENTURY, **HALT!** WE'RE HAVING A BREAK!

THE QUICKER WE FIND TRAGICOMIX THE BETTER FOR PANACEA...

I DON'T WANT HER TO WORRY...

26A

D'YOU THINK IT'LL BE EASY TO FIND TRAGICOMIX?

HEY! YOU TWO! I SAID WE'RE HAVING A BREAK!

LET'S HOPE SO, OBELIX!

NO TIME! COME ON! COME ON!

BUT I'M GIVING THE ORDERS AROUND HERE! THIS IS A BREAK! HEY, THIS IS A BREAK...

YOU GO AHEAD! WE'RE GOING ON!

THAT WAS A GOOD ONE, THAT WAS!

WELL, HOW'S THIS FOR ATTIC SALT? OUR CENTURION'S ZEUSLESS!

THAT'D LAY THEM IN THE ISLES, OLD BOY!

I'm not sure just how to put that in Gothic and Egyptian, but I'll do my best...

!!!

CRAZY! THEY'RE CRAZY! THEY'RE ACTUALLY EAGER TO GO INTO BATTLE!

PAF!

26B

THE COLUMN OF THE 1ST LEGION, 3RD COHORT, 2ND MANIPLE, 1ST CENTURY IS STILL ON THE GO BUT HAS UNDERGONE A SLIGHT MODIFICATION AS TO MARCHING ORDER...

HALT! WE'LL CAMP HERE FOR TONIGHT!

ER... UM... RIGHT! DIG A DITCH ROUND THE SITE... BUILD A STOCKADE! PITCH YOUR TENTS AROUND YOUR CENTURION'S TENT! ORGANISE SENTRY DUTY...

I SHOULDN'T BOTHER. LOOK AT 'EM!

POF! POF!

27A

!!!

TONIGHT'S MENU: BOAR ON THE SPIT AND GÂTEAU Á LA CRÈME

SUITS ME!

I'LL HAVE MY BOAR MEDIUM RARE, PLEASE.

WHILE THEIR MEN ARE STUFFING THEMSELVES, THE TWO ROMAN OFFICERS MAKE DO WITH THE FRUGAL REGULATION MEAL IN THEIR SMALL REGULATION TENT...

HONK! SCRONTCH! SLIP! SLOP! SCRITCH MIAM!

AFTER A SHORT NIGHT'S SLEEP ...

YAWN!

?

NEFARIUS PURPUS!

THEY'VE GONE!

27B

THE BARRACKS ARE IN THE NEW PORT. JUST A WORD OF ADVICE, BY JUPITER! GET YOURSELVES SMARTENED UP! IF YOU GO ABOUT MASSILIA DRESSED UP LIKE THAT YOU'LL SOON GET A DRESSING DOWN!

SOON AFTERWARDS IN THE OFFICES OF THE COMMANDING TRIBUNE OF THE MASSILIA BARRACKS...

OH YES, YOU'RE THE REINFORCEMENTS FROM CONDATUM ... THE GALLEY'S WAITING. YOU CAN GO ON BOARD. JULIUS CAESAR'S ENCAMPED NEAR THAPSUS, WAITING TO ATTACK.

HERE'S OUR GALLEY!

KEEP RANKS! KEEP QUIET... PLEASE KEEP QUIET!

CENTURION NEFARIUS PURPUS, READY TO LEAVE WHEN THE TIDE ALLOWS!

29A

WHAT DID THAT MAN SAY?

OLD HAIRY EYEBROWS.

HAHAHAHA!

I SEE! WE'RE A FEW OARSMEN SHORT. EXERCISE WILL KEEP THEM QUIET!

NOTHING WILL KEEP THIS LOT QUIET, CAPTAIN ...NOTHING WILL KEEP THEM QUIET!

LET GO AFT!

WH...WHAT D'YOU MEAN, LET GO AFT?

THERE SHE GOES!

HE SAID...

I KNOW, I KNOW... OLD HAIRY NOSE.

29B

JULIUS CAESAR'S TENT...

SCIPIO IS LYING IN WAIT TO THE NORTH, JUBA 1ST, KING OF NUMIDIA, AND THE TRAITOR AFRANIUS TO THE SOUTH. WE CAN THEREFORE SEE THAT OUR POSITION...

?

WHO ARE YOU? HOW DARE YOU ENTER CAESAR'S TENT?

ARE YOU THERE, PTENISNET?

WHAT'S THIS MAN SAYING?

HE... ER, HE WANTS TO KNOW IF YOU'RE ONE OF THE RED-CLOAKS... ER, ONE OF THE HOLIDAY CAMP HELPERS... WHAT SORT OF ACTIVITIES YOU... ER...

GET OUT!

33A

AS I WAS SAYING, WE ARE IN A SERIOUS POSITION. ON WHICH FRONT DO WE ATTACK? TO THE NORTH, OR...

NO, THAT'S NOT A BAR, I DON'T THINK WE'LL FIND ANY BEER IN HERE!

AWFULLY SORRY! WE SAW THIS BIG TENT, AND WE THOUGHT IT MIGHT BE...

GET OUT, BY JUPITER!!!

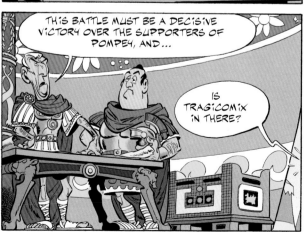

THIS BATTLE MUST BE A DECISIVE VICTORY OVER THE SUPPORTERS OF POMPEY, AND...

IS TRAGICOMIX IN THERE?

WHO THE DEVIL ARE ALL THESE PEOPLE?

1ST LEGION, 3RD COHORT, 2ND MANIPLE, 1ST CENTURY. AVE!

33B

41

42

WE HAVE ALREADY BEEN PRIVILEGED TO SHOW YOU ROMAN LEGIONARIES ENGAGED IN MANOEUVRES. WE NOW HAVE THE ADDITIONAL PLEASURE OF PRESENTING ROMAN LEGIONARIES ENGAGED IN MANOEUVRES AGAINST ROMAN LEGIONARIES...

FORM A PHALANX!

FORM A QUINCUNX!

FORM A TORTOISE!

FORM A SQUARE!

FORM A CIRCLE!

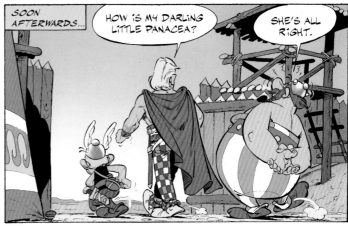